KILLER AT DARK HOLLOW LAKE

K. MOORE

ISBN-13: 978-1-7328844-9-6

ONE

The small town and its surrounding suburbs look extremely typical. People are out, walking along the tree-lined footpaths, going about their everyday activities. In their minds, nothing seems amiss. They'd be asking themselves all the standard questions, like: *Did I turn the oven off? Will he ask me out on a date today? Should I get a double shot of coffee in my latte before heading to the office?* Mundane things.

I drive through the streets, slightly envious of their naïveté as to what goes on behind closed doors in the shadowy hours of the night. Oblivious to the dark, where monsters that lurk are unleashed and given permission to play.

What makes a monster? This question is one I've found myself continually asking. Are they the product of nature or nurture? The debate between academics is ongoing, just a lot of speculation and data that could support either or both arguments. Some say it's a genetic tendency toward violence mixed with an abusive childhood that makes a killer cocktail resulting in such evil; others disagree.

Manicured lawns and colorful garden beds are the first things I notice as I pull in front of the house. That, and the yellow door. It's a welcoming house, both happy and cheerful. Or it would be if it wasn't for the yellow tape and the uniformed policemen blocking the view of a few bystanders. Hopefully5 I've made it before the crime scene technician has processed the evidence and the coroner's called to take the body to the morgue. As gruesome as it sounds, I want to see the dead in person and not have to rely on photos or laboratory reports.

My car door slams. I adjust my jacket, ensuring my gun is concealed before I reach into my pocket to pull out my badge. I need to gain access to the property quickly before any press arrives and notes my presence. The last thing the local sheriff's office needs is speculation as to why an FBI agent is in town. And the last thing I need is for my boss to find out I'm at the scene of what I believe to be the sixth murder of a serial killer. It's more than a hunch on my behalf. I've studied the data and isolated the similarities. It's also my job.

With a flick of the wrist to show my badge and after donning blue plastic shoe covers to protect the gruesome evidence, I'm given access with barely an eyebrow raised. After I was alerted to the situation, the short conversation I had on the phone with the deputy provided me with the rundown on the victim. She was reportedly single and lived alone. No evidence of forced entry, and the feminine interior of the house is as neat and tidy as the front yard. Framed photos hanging on the hallway wall show a pretty blonde with a beautiful smile. Some were taken with an older couple who look like her parents. I wonder if the sheriff's department has notified them yet.

I take a deep breath and step into the main bedroom. A technician looks up but goes back to dusting furniture for prints once he sees the badge I've hooked on my belt. The other is carefully taking photos of the victim. She's naked but half-covered by the bed linen. Her body is curled onto its right side, almost in a fetal position, with her hands together, as though she were praying. Her wrists show evidence of rope burn, and her neck exhibits telltale bruising. It's almost exactly the same as the others.

"Have you been able to ascertain the time of death?" I ask the room.

The guy taking the photos stops and turns. "We can't be certain until we get her back to the morgue, but we think at least forty-eight hours."

Not long at all. Some of the other victims weren't discovered as quickly. I watch the technicians go about their work. They're being thorough, which is good. Not all jurisdictions where the other murders occurred were processed with the same level of care. It definitely has made my job harder to try and convince people of the commonality between them when evidence hasn't been reported correctly or has been compromised.

"Has the body been moved, or was she killed in here?" I bend over and take a look at the wrist burns. They're raw but not seeping, nor have they scabbed over.

The killer mustn't have subdued her long before he killed her.

"As far as we can tell, she was killed here."

I nod and leave them to their work to take a look around the rest of the house, confident the forensic report will hold all the technical information needed. The bathroom doesn't exhibit the same neat vibe as the rest of the house. The hamper is filled, and I pull on a pair of gloves before lifting a few items. Outdoor activity clothes. This matches with the deputy's briefing of her having been away on leave. There's a towel pushed under the sink as well as one hanging on the drying rack. I lift the one from the floor and bring it to my nose. It's still damp.

Did the killer have a shower before or after he took her life?

"Can you process the bathroom as well?" I say, walking back into the bedroom. "There's a towel on the floor that the killer might have used."

"Sure thing."

There's got to be something else. Something else to tie this murder to the one I'm interested in. I know what it is but need something substantial to point me in the right direction. The killer is undeniably careful, not wanting to leave any evidence to his or her identity. Everything I have to prove this body is just the latest number in a string of murders tied to one killer is circumstantial.

The kitchen is at the back of the house, overlooking a small courtyard. Again, it's cozy and feminine with potted plants showcasing bursts of color. The victim obviously took pride in her house. No dishes in the sink or Chinese takeout cartons in the trash. I pick up the camera charging on the counter and power it on. With care, I flick through the files one at a time.

They're of her recent vacation, the last photo taken only three days ago. I stop at one image and enlarge it, focusing on the sign in the top-right corner.

Dark Hollow Lake Diner.

Reading off the numbered filenames, I realize they're not in sequence. Photos have been deleted. Carefully studying the images on either side of the missing photos, I take note of the locations, looking for any additional clues. Scenes of rock pools and a waterfall preface eight missing images, followed by a blurry photo of the ground … and a dark brown hiking boot attached to a hairy, muscular leg.

Got him.

TWO

Her scent is gone.

THREE

The computer makes a final beep before the screen goes black. I look at the two pieces of paper next to the keyboard and sigh. It's all that's left of my notes on the cases I've been working on for the past six months. With me taking my last-minute leave, the work's been handed over to one of the new analysts, newly out of training. The little upstart didn't even want my handover notes, too enthusiastic to dive in with fresh eyes. I wonder if I had the same annoying level of exuberance when I was green.

All that's left for me is to shred them, and then I can go home to finish packing for my month off. Having visited the last kill location, I'm more than eager to leave.

Chair wheels squeak as I push back away from the desk and look at the blank walls of my cubicle. It lacks personality now that notes and maps have been taken down even though my colleagues would argue that it was always dull and boring. Prim and proper. No personal photos of boyfriends, pets, or children have ever graced my walls. Not even selfies in those standard cool poses.

That's what happens when you're married to the job. Life outside doesn't exist. It becomes all of those things to you, and after a while, the missing colorful charisma doesn't even rate. All that matters is the work—supporting the field agents to catch the bad guy and close the cases.

It's why I joined the FBI. Why I'm taking leave now.

"Jamie, you're all packed up? Excited about your time off?" My boss, August—or Auggie, as he likes to be called—leans against the partition separating the space from my neighbors.

I try not to look at the files with the thick red classification stamps on the outside. Instead, I shrug and plaster the smile on my face, attempting to suck down the guilt of lies I'm about to tell.

"Of course. It's been a hectic few years. I'm so grateful you gave me the time to get away and recharge."

"Burnout is real, my friend. Are you doing anything special?" he asks, raising an eyebrow. "Did I miss the travel request application?"

"No, sir. I'm staying domestic. Heading into the mountains. Nothing but hiking trails, pristine lakes, and unpolluted fresh air … and a trunkload of novels that have been gathering dust over the past few years. Time to relax and catch up on my reading of the nonfiction variety."

Auggie laughs. He, more so than anyone else in our department, knows the hours I've been putting in over the past twelve months. I'm always first in and last to leave and never seen without those manila folders in my arms when my nose isn't buried in the online versions.

I'm the branch's top analyst; not much gets by me. And that's been the issue as of late and the reason why I was asked to take some time off. I jumped at the opportunity because of murder scenes like the one I visited yesterday.

"I just need to shred these, and I'll officially be out of your hair for the next few weeks." I stand with the mass of papers held in my hands.

He reaches across and takes the paperwork. "I can do that for you. Call it a final parting favor."

I shrug. "You sure you're going to be able to cope without me?"

"I won't lie. We'll miss you, but I think it'll do you good to take a break. Too much of all this"—he waves the files in his hands and gestures around the room— "is not healthy for anyone."

"I'm sure you're right," I say with a tight smile. "Well, if you're going to take care of that, then I'm out of here."

The cubicle darkens with a simple flick of the switch.

I pick up my leather satchel and hook it over my shoulder. "Thanks, Auggie. I'll see you in a few weeks."

―――――――――

The keys clink on the entrance table in the darkened corridor of my apartment. Knowing the layout by rote, I don't bother with the lights. Not that it's difficult since I only own the bare minimum compared to societal norms. I never really saw the need to buy a bunch of stuff to decorate my living space in line with a Martha Stewart photo shoot. Dust collectors—that's what all of the additional things would be. Plus, I don't entertain or have visitors, so I only have to cater to myself, just the way I like it.

Five steps in, I drop my bag on the kitchen bench and open the fridge to grab a beer. After popping the top, I take another seven steps and drop down onto the single leather recliner in what the building plans would earmark as the living room of this small one-bed, one-bath studio apartment. I kick the footrest up, toeing my mid-height heels off in the process, and turn the switch on for the lamp beside me before taking a long pull of the cool amber liquid. I smile as the wall in front of me illuminates with my most secret obsession.

Yellow and pink Post-it Notes surround pinned photos and newspaper articles splayed around a large map. The photos are clumped together in groups, each of them showcasing one section of a gruesome scene. Specific body parts are the common thread between them all—wrists burned and marred from being bound too tight by rope and blue-green strangulation marks around the necks. Each of the collective groupings is of women who were found dead in their houses over the past two years. Each in a different state. And each a victim to what I believe is the same killer.

These murders have remained unsolved after the investigations were carried out by local law enforcement. Since none are in the same jurisdiction or the same state, no one has looked at them as a whole and pegged them for what they are.

Except for me.

Green string runs from each external small nucleus of images and notes across to a large black thumbtack—the murder locations. Six of those tacks launch red strings across the map, following the trail of clues left by the killer, to meet smack-bang in the center of a secluded lake resort community deep in the Tennessee Valley area of the Smoky Mountains.

Dark Hollow Lake—the nexus point of commonality between each of the murders.

Laid out like this, the evidence is damning. Unfortunately, the FBI doesn't agree.

Analytical findings—my findings—the FBI refuses to consider to be what I believe is a murderous spree by a serial killer.

I upend the beer and drain its contents before standing. Carefully, I start disassembling the link chart and collating its items into envelopes. These will be coming on vacation with me, packed alongside my dusty, unread collection of last year's best sellers, hiking boots, and my 9mm pistol.

Dark Hollow Lake—my working holiday destination.

Now, the investigation can really begin.

FOUR

Roses.
    She tasted like roses.
Coated in the predawn dew.
Like her name.
But her fragrance is now no more.
Two in two weeks.
Roses are sweet.

FIVE

The GPS said it was four hundred eighty-three miles to my final destination and that it would take me roughly nine and a half hours. I didn't believe it. It looked pretty much like a straight line from start to finish. How wrong could a person be? I'm just thankful I had the foresight to start early to miss the city commuter traffic.

The scenery change from Virginia to Tennessee has been breathtaking. It almost makes me feel guilty that my trip to the area has ulterior motives. Almost.

But then I think of the women whose lives were taken too early. How they must have felt while driving this route or one similar, more than likely looking for an adventure. Hunting for outdoor activities, coupled with the Hallmark experience of a slower-paced town, a retreat from reality and all of its bureaucratic overtures. I grimace, thinking of my office and Auggie. Maybe the latter issue is only mine. Either way, these women hadn't signed up for what they got when they returned to their normal life.

Not at all. But I do know that I'm here to make certain it doesn't happen again.

I'm not sure how I linked the first two murders together; there was just a familiarity with them that pulled me to look a bit closer. And when a third unsolved murder was reported a few months later, showcasing similar modus operandi, of course, I took it to my boss. Serial killer motivations—what makes a serial killer and what it is they're after—was one of the items we spent time studying while at Quantico.

By identifying an emerging killer, I could potentially stop future murders and solve the spate of unsolved cases across multiple states. And I could cement my place in the bureau, get a promotion, and rub it into the faces of all the naysayers who told me I was crazy to pursue this.

I found it troubling that no one was interested in my findings and no one would listen. Auggie would plaster on his fake-ass smile and nod as I spoke before dismissing me. Even my coworkers thought I was crazy, too many late nights in front of a computer screen affecting my judgment. Overworked and burned out.

But it's there. It's in the data. I've been trained to see the patterns, something I excel at. And regardless of my impeccable record of pulling Hail Marys to solve the unsolvable in the past, no one believes that there's a serial killer afoot.

But it's okay … he won't be for long.

I brake slowly, come to a stop, place the car out of gear, and pull the hand brake in front of Dark Hollow Lake Diner. I'm dead on my feet, and if I'm going to make it to the cabin I rented, I'll need caffeine. And directions.

The atmosphere as I push through the front doors is calming. The smell of coffee permeates through the air with the scent of seared meat.

Several of the booths are taken.

A cute guy in his early thirties, wearing a plaid shirt behind the counter, waves to me. "Take a seat. I'll be with you in a minute."

He turns to grab two plates topped with burgers and fries and heads to the women in the far corner booth. My stomach rumbles at the sight of the food. I can't remember when it was that I last stopped for gas and scarfed down that disgusting gas-station hot dog.

Maybe I'll get some food too.

I take a seat and pick up the menu, not to decide what I want to eat because those meals I saw sealed the deal for me. No, I want to see what else they offer since my research showed the town only had two diners and a pub. Not being much of a cook means I need to rely on others to prepare my meals. I'll also need to be out and seen for the investigative work, so I might as well familiarize myself with my surroundings as much as I can.

"Hi there. I'm Luke," he says. "What can I get you?"

"I'll just take a coffee and one of those burgers, thanks."

"Sure thing." He walks away and hangs the ticket over the small opening separating the kitchen from the dining area. "Order up, Hal."

He returns with a mug and the coffeepot. "Creamers are on the table. Give me a holler if you need anything else."

I take a sip of the dark liquid, appreciating its strength, and pull out the paperwork I compiled, containing my cabin booking and details of this town. It's not a particularly large town, which makes sense, as it's quite a stretch away from any major cities or infrastructure. The area boasts a healthy tourist turnover with skiing in winter and outdoor activities in summer. Founded as a remote trade outpost for fur trappers in the mid-eighteenth century and then rumored to be a runaway slave sanctuary during the Civil War, the population here has always remained small with increases being of a short-term nature.

The perfect place for a psychopathic serial killer to live unnoticed.

"Here's your burger." A huge mound with melted cheese oozing from the side is placed on the table to my left. "Ah, you must be Jamie. We were expecting you to pass through. I think I should offer up an apology on behalf of the town. We thought you were Jamie, boy, not Jamie, girl."

I look up to him incredulously. How could he possibly know who I was? At my obviously confused expression, his smile widens into a full grin.

"You've got to understand," he says with a chuckle, "it's a small town, and that there sheet of paper has an image of ol' Bobby's Whiskey Trail Cabin. He was in yesterday, chattin' about how you'd be staying with us for a few weeks."

My mouth must drop to the floor with this revelation. Too bad for my quiet infiltration of the town and its people, not that it would've lasted long once I started asking questions. I'm sure my activities while in town will not mirror those of a normal tourist. A cover story might have been a wiser move, but covert operations have never been my strong suit.

However, following the threads and finding the links absolutely is.

"Yep, that's me. Here to unwind for some much-needed R&R." I sit back and let my shoulders relax into the booth's cushions. "But this is great because if you know the Whiskey Trail Cabin, you can give me directions."

"Sure can. For now, enjoy your burger. Let me know if there's something else I can get for you, and I'll be back when you're done to give you those directions."

He turns and walks away as I sigh. If what Luke said is true, then everybody will know who I am and who I work for very soon. That means the killer—if he's as smart as I think he is—will also know why I'm here. A smile breaks out on my face at the thought of identifying him.

Picking up the burger with two hands, I take my first bite.

The Whiskey Trail Cabin is a few miles out of town, and even with my GPS, I'm not sure if I would've found it without the trail identifiers Luke gave me at the diner. "Burning man" and "alien mound" made no sense until I hit the gravel road that brought me here.

It's not that far from Main Street, but at the same time, it's remote. Large glass windows frame a picturesque view of nothing but greenery. This would be a perfect getaway for anyone wanting to disconnect from everything for a while. Pity I have more pressing matters at hand.

The cabin is modestly furnished with all of the regular conveniences, but the only things that interests me is the bedrooms. There are two of them nestled behind the open kitchen and lounge area, but since I'm the sole person here, I only have access to the main one. I throw the smaller of my bags onto the double bed and walk through the connected bathroom to the adjoining door. It's locked, as expected, but it doesn't take much more than a few jiggles with my lock-picking equipment, and I'm in.

With deft movements, I unzip the case at my feet and get to work. Thick tape pins blackout material in place to cover the window, and I run my fingers over the edges to make sure no space will let out light. I set about rearranging the room to give me unobstructed access to the far wall by pushing the twin beds out of the way.

The cabin remains silent while I re-create a version of my investigation board; the process is calming. Each photo I tape up cements my resolve that coming here was the right thing. The perpetrator shouldn't get away with this, but more importantly, he shouldn't be allowed to kill again. I need to stop him.

I'm more than confident with my profiling and analytical abilities, and I'm sure he'll be easy enough to sniff out. He's probably a white male in his early thirties with a seasonal or flexible job. Someone who more than likely grew up with a single parent and spent his youth looking for validation.

In a small town where everyone apparently knows everyone, he must have slipped up; someone must have seen something. I just need to find that someone to find him.

After a few more minutes of staring at the board, I head back into my room to unpack and sort through my belongings. Tomorrow's going to be interesting.

SIX

Hello, Jamie.
  I see you.
At the diner, flirting with Luke.
Why do you feel the need to flirt?
With Luke?
Will you flirt with me?
Our flirtation would be so sweet.
Like you.
I can't wait to taste it.

SEVEN

It was weird, waking up to a lack of sound. Uncomfortable even. The cabin had an eerie calmness in its silence, and it only took me a few minutes to dress and lock up before hightailing it back into town. I could have stayed at one of the hotels or a local Airbnb, but I wanted my privacy and the extra space. Surrounded by nothing but earth, sky, and forest certainly meets that need. It doesn't take me long to head in search of food.

Luke greets me with a smile as I enter the diner and take a seat in the same booth as yesterday. It's bustling this morning, obviously a popular breakfast locale, and I covertly study the other patrons over the top of my menu. One of them could be the killer. More probable is that someone in this room knows the killer and doesn't even realize it.

"Good morning, Jamie," Luke says as he places a coffee in front of me. "What can I get you?"

"Just your breakfast special and some advice when you have a few minutes free, please."

"Sure thing. I'll be right back."

I watch as he goes from table to table, sharing pleasantries and refreshing the beverages. No wonder he knew who I was yesterday; everyone really does know everyone here. I can probably use this information to my advantage. It might make my job of trying to sniff out a killer much easier, maybe even flush him out.

In my study of the other patrons, I'm left wondering if any of them could be capable of murdering those women. They all appear so normal, but that's one of the superpowers of a serial killer.

"Here you go." With my breakfast in hand, Luke slides into the booth across from me. "Now, what can I help you with?"

I drag the plate across while I contemplate my game plan. I need to meet with the sheriff. I know who he is from having called him more than a couple times over the past few months. He'll have an idea of why I'm here even if he won't agree with me. Sheriff Layton always came across as very competent and a stickler for protocol. I also believe he's loyal to the community and he'll do whatever it takes to keep them safe.

"What can you tell me about the sheriff?" I ask Luke before popping a piece of bacon in my mouth.

"Dan Layton? He's been sheriff here for a while now. Grew up around these parts. Solid, smart, and doesn't stand for much nonsense."

I nod. This mirrors the mental picture I drew from my dealings with him over the phone. The first call I'd made was to have him verify some information almost eighteen months ago.

Luke leans in, elbows on the table, and whispers, "You got a problem requiring the sheriff already?"

His concern is endearing, and I stop myself from laughing at his question.

"No," I reply just as quietly. "I'm with the bureau, and I have spoken to him once or twice over the phone. I thought I'd go say hello in person."

"I thought you had that government look about you," Luke says shrewdly. "Dan knows this town and has a finger on the pulse. It's good you're going to see him because he'd probably work out who you were and come find you. Not much goes on here without his knowing about it."

Perfect.

Now, to convince him that the killer of these women is one of his own.

I leave the diner and decide to walk up Main Street to the sheriff's office. It's a beautiful day, and I can see why such a small town boasts the tourist numbers it does. Not too many, just the ones who want to seemingly get off-grid for a while. The town has maintained the charm a lot of places lose from growing too large or upgrading to more modern conveniences or franchises.

Walking through the glass doors, I stop at the counter and wait for the front-desk clerk to notice me. She looks up at me in greeting.

"Good morning. I was hoping to see Sheriff Layton, if that's at all possible?" I ask with a smile.

"Yes, ma'am," she drawls. "Is he expectin' ya?"

"No." I keep my answer short and to the point. No need to elaborate; it'll only stir gossip, and I'm not ready for that just yet. It's best if the details of my visit and who I am come from the sheriff himself.

"Bet you're that FBI lady stayin' up at Bobby's, huh?"

Well, crap. Gotta love that small-town charm.

I sigh and extend my hand. "Yes. Jamie Rogers. But I'm not here on official business."

She chews the inside of her lip and flicks a stray hair behind her ear while studying me. "Aight then. I'll go tell him yer here."

She pushes back from the table to stand and ambles past the partition. Shortly after, she reappears and waves me through by pointing to the door at the far end of the mainly open-plan office. Before I get a chance to knock, the door's opened by a tall man with cropped ginger hair.

"Special Agent Rogers? Come in and take a seat." He shuts the door after I cross the threshold and moves to the seat behind the large mahogany desk. "What can I do for you?"

"It's Jamie, and first off, it's great to finally meet you in person. I appreciate the information you've provided to me at the bureau over the past year or so."

"Yes. Yes, those were unfortunate cases. Is that why you're here today?" He sits back in his chair and crosses his arms, coming straight to the point of my visit.

"That's a hard one to answer," I say honestly, leaning forward. "I want to say yes, but I can't. I'm officially on leave, but …"

"If you had something—if the bureau had something—then you'd be here officially," he says, not missing a beat. "I know you've been calling about these women …"

I'm about to interject, but his raised hand momentarily silences me.

"And, yes," he continues, "the ones you've called about were all here at one point or another on vacation. But what you need to realize is that this is a popular tourist spot. We get many people passing through at all times of the year for all sorts of reasons."

"I realize that." My words come out a little too harshly, and I take a deep breath to calm myself before continuing, "I just really think there's something going on here. I can feel it. Some things aren't adding up, and I want the opportunity to look around and work out what it is."

There's a moment of uncomfortable silence. Sheriff Layton sucks his lip between his teeth, picks up a pen, and taps it while staring out the window. I follow his gaze into the parking lot adjacent to the building as a blue Dodge pulls in.

"If what you are saying is true ..." he starts softly, looking back to me with cautious eyes. "If what you say is true, that means one of the residents here is the killer."

"Yes, I'm afraid that's what the evidence points to. I could be wrong, but I won't know unless I run through a few leads."

He doesn't move but continues to study me. I decide to go with my gut and be completely transparent as to what my intentions are. My gut has never led me astray to date.

"I'm planning on following up on a few leads." He opens his mouth to say something, but I continue quickly, not letting him speak, "I'm not going to do anything that will jeopardize any of your investigations or that will put you in an awkward spot with the members of the town or the FBI. That's the last thing I want to do. Before you say anything, let me tell you everything about my analysis and theories because I want to move forward with your blessing."

If I can get him to hear me out, I know I can convince him. I know I've won the first battle when he sighs and nods for me to continue. Now, to convince him that Dark Hollow Lake is the linchpin linking these murders.

The sheriff rubs his temples. With pursed lips, he flips over the last of the photos as I finish up my brief before he raises his head to study me.

"I can see why you came." He closes the file and sits back in the chair, exhaling loudly before running a hand through his buzz cut.

I remain silent, watching his internal struggle as he comes to grips with everything he just saw and heard.

"I'm glad you came in and let me know why you're in town," he says slowly. "I'll keep my eyes and ears to the ground. This is a small town. Maybe your presence will stir things up, but I sure hope it doesn't. I'd hate to think someone here was responsible for something this gruesome."

"Thanks, Sheriff. I'll keep you updated if I uncover anything."

I stand and offer my hand across the desk.

"Make sure you do. And, Jamie … be careful."

The door to his office closes behind me, and I smile at the two uniformed deputies standing by the water cooler. They greet me with a nod and return to their conversation, ignoring the two sullen handcuffed teenagers sitting opposite a desk holding multiple cans of spray paint. The office is bustling compared to when I arrived. Outside, the weather is still lovely.

"Here you go, ma'am." The driver of the Dodge steps to the side to hold the door open and lets me pass.

"Thanks."

He waves off my thanks and disappears to the front.

EIGHT

You smell so fresh.
    Is it the starch in your clothes?
Or the shampoo you used to wash your hair this morning?
    Garnier Fructis Pure Clean Shampoo.
    With aloe extract and vitamin E.
    My fingers still linger with your scent.
    I like the way you smiled at me.

NINE

The cool breeze sweeping from the lake across the well-worn pier offers a respite from the thickened humidity trapped among the buildings of the town. Ripples from an invisible disturbance gently lap against the moss-stained pilings. With the images from the latest victim to guide me, I stand in front of the aged lakeside building. Peeling strips of color indicate brighter times.

A shiver goes down my spine, and I shrug deeper into my denim jacket before looking around. Other than a woman pushing a stroller a few hundred feet away from me along the path, there's no one else about. As nonsensical as it seems, I've this weird sense that someone's watching me, my body feeling heavy under the weight from the unseen set of eyes. Reluctantly, I shake it off and bring my mind back to the task at hand—finding a killer.

The screen door snaps shut with a muted, metallic thud behind me as I enter the run-down shack and am greeted by a face from the diner. Earlier this morning, he was seated with a young woman and girl, sharing breakfast.

"Can I help you?"

The name tag on the dirty green work shirt identifies him as Xander. Fins, masks, and snorkels hang from hooks on the adjacent wall, supposedly sorted by size. I ignore them and scan the rest of the room. A large map surrounded by framed images behind the counter catches my attention, and I take a few steps toward it.

"Maybe," I say noncommittally in answer to his question.

"Got some snorkeling tours later this week. Don't know what yer into. A lot of folks check out the Fort Sevier Ruins. It's like an underwater ghost town." He chuckles at his own joke.

"Indeed," I say, studying the photos. The one with a water rushing over large stones is familiar, and I point toward it. "Where's this one taken?"

"Ahh," he says, moving closer. "That's near the outlet for Ratchet's Creek. It runs alongside Ratchet's Pass and has a few pooled areas before it feeds into the lake. It's almost straight across from here. Not too far away from the ruins. That there photo's old. You can't get there by boat 'cause of the debris, but you can still get there on foot."

He moves behind the antique counter to retrieve a pamphlet and folds it open, pen in hand. I move closer, interested in what he's about to show me.

"Here's an old visitor map. It's out of date with some information, but none of the hiking trails or sightseeing locations have changed. What's not on here though is Ratchet's Pass. The trailhead is about five miles from town ... about here." He marks a spot on the map before drawing a curved line and circling an area on the edge of the lake. "It's sort of off the beaten track, mainly used by locals and not as maintained like these others. The only way now to get to that location"—he nods toward the photo board—"is to walk or run the six miles to it. It's not easy, but it might be worth it."

He shrugs and puts the pen down. I cast my gaze back to the image on the wall and mentally compare it to the one I'm thinking of from the latest victim's camera. Hers could've been taken anywhere, as I'm sure rocks and streams aren't that uncommon in these parts. It's more a hunch than anything else when I ask my next question.

"Are there any waterfalls in the area by chance?"

Xander smiles and taps on an area between his notations. "Sure is, right about here. It only really runs after the rain, and when it does, it's not that safe on that particular trail. When you get to the point where the trail splits, you can either head up to the top of the pass and trek down to the waterfall or follow the creek line back to find it."

He folds the map and hands it to me. "Now, can I interest you in a snorkeling trip? Visibility's perfect at the moment."

I sigh and shake my head. As tempting as it is, I'm not really here on vacation. I've work to do, and I am not too sure if this small, close-knit town is going to hinder or help my queries. Once I start asking questions, everyone will get an idea of why I'm really here.

Xander's currently sporting flip-flops with his jean cutoffs, but that doesn't mean he can't own a pair of hiking boots. His in-depth knowledge—identifying one of my areas of interest—is helpful, but realistically, I suppose most, if not all, locals would know of the area. I study Xander's profile; his dark hair, beard, and hazel eyes, coupled with his easygoing nature, would definitely make him attractive to women. I wonder if he's the type of guy to go after the attention of tourists.

"No. I'm trying to trace the steps of a woman who was in town last month," I say, watching him closely. "She supposedly was into water activities, and I need to know if she took any trips out on the lake."

Xander straightens his posture, and his eyes narrow as he shrewdly studies me. "You're that FBI lady they've been talking about at Luke's."

I grimace slightly, wondering if I should've created a cover story before arriving in town. I knew it was a small town; I just didn't count on it being so prone to gossip.

"Have you always worked here?" I say, ignoring his question.

He nods and drags a large leather-bound book down from the bench in front of him. "Yep. I've owned this outfit for a few years now." He shrugs. "It's only operational during the summer though, for obvious reasons."

I step closer as he opens what must be the reservation diary.

"Do you have a name? I realize it's a bit old school, but we keep all of the booking details in here."

"Yes. Dawn Chapman."

Xander lifts his head, and his eyes meet mine. "I remember Dawn. She was something. It's not often we hit it off with the tourists, but she was a lotta fun. Here on her own. She came to a few of the local bonfire parties down on the lake." He closes the book without looking at it and chuckles. "She had a few of the boys here fighting for her attention. Knew how to hold her liquor too. Yeah, great girl."

I ponder the shared information, mentally going through all the details I have on Chapman. There were no images on her camera of any bonfires. Either she didn't take the expensive piece of equipment to the gatherings or they were among the ones deleted. Considering her body—the way it was found and with no visible forced entry into the house ... she must have known and was comfortable with her killer. Probably even intimate.

Or not.

It could be possible that the killer was jealous of her intimacy with someone else.

"Were you one of the guys fighting over her, Xander?"

"No." He pauses a moment, brows furrowed. "What's this about? If this has something to do with her credit card being overcharged, we fixed all of that."

Interesting.

He fidgets uncomfortably, and I remain silent, observing him.

"I know," I finally say, bluffing—not wanting to explain the exact details of why I'm here. "How well did you get to know her, Xander?"

"I don't know. I didn't hang out with her much," he says quickly, shaking his head. "I took her on a snorkeling tour of the ruins that one day, and she came back a few days later, questioning the charges. But I fixed all of that up straightaway for her. Otherwise, I only saw her a few times at the tavern when I was on shift or at some of the local parties, either with Jayson or Conners."

Jayson and Conners.

I lock those two names away. The killer had to have been close to her for her to share personal details, like her home address. Unless he was able to get it another way—from the resort … or from a banking institution. I make a mental note to follow up on the so-called mistaken charges, wondering if it's the perfect excuse to get personal information from a customer.

"Who are they?" I ask, referring to the names he eagerly shared.

His nervousness subsides slightly with the question, taking us away from the overpayment issue.

"Jay does maintenance work for the ski lodge and resort. He's also one of the senior volunteer firefighters. He helps ol' Marty—head of the fire department—out regularly. Conners works for the sheriff. He's not from around here—transferred in a few years back after splitting with his wife."

Conners.

He could have been one of the deputies by the water cooler this morning. I wonder which one, trying to recall the physical attributes of the two men I saw. Him moving after a marital breakup is an interesting fact and worth following up on, as it's not uncommon for psychopaths to focus in on and try to replicate monstrosities from their past.

"And Dawn was dating one of them?"

Xander laughs and shakes his head. "They wish. Nah, she was just a cool chick. Fun to hang out with. I don't think she was looking for a boyfriend."

I nod, not wanting to make it obvious where my interest lies. "So, the charge issue was all sorted?"

"Yeah, it was. All a misunderstanding." Xander looks away quickly, nervously flicking the corner of the diary.

"Okay. Thanks for the information," I say, turning to leave. "See you around."

My steps are light after exiting the dive store.

Two names.

I've now got two names.

"You're off to a good start, Rogers," I congratulate myself on a whisper.

TEN

Did you sense me, Jamie?
Don't fret.
It won't be long.

ELEVEN

Confident with my new leads, I'm heading back to the diner for lunch when my phone rings. The name on the screen has me pulling over to the side of the road. Hesitantly, I swipe to connect the call and sit back, closing my eyes.

"Auggie," I say as pleasantly as possible.

It's my first full day in town, and I can't help but feel like I've been busted by the school principal, doing something wrong. If he knows what I'm really doing here, he'll likely demand I leave and return to work to face some sort of disciplinary action. We might be federal agents, but we're still required to follow the rules and direction of our superiors.

"Jamie. Just checking in. I know it's only been a few days." His voice sounds slightly harried. It's probably not discernible to others, and it's only due to how close-knit our section is that I can hear it.

"It has been. But that's not why you're calling. What's up?"

He chuckles. "You can see right through me, can't you?"

Auggie goes on to explain how the new analyst misplaced or mislabeled a case file and asked if I kept a backup of my notes in the system. Relief washes over me as he describes the conversation he had with the little upstart. I feel vindicated about my initial thoughts of him and silently hope he learns from this. We're all part of a team and need to work together.

Except when one steps out and does one's own thing, I think, cringing. *Am I any better, hunting a could-be serial killer on my time off?*

"Oh, there was one other thing," Auggie says after I explain where he could access my notes. "Your name's been flagged. Someone ran it through the police database. The query came from Dark Hollow Lake Sheriff's Department."

Oh shit.

My finger involuntarily taps on the steering wheel while I quickly analyze his words. His tone didn't give anything away this time. I decide to play it casual and offer up some information, as close to the truth that I can.

"That makes sense. Dark Hollow Lake's a small town, and I was called out as government on arrival. I dropped by the sheriff's department earlier today to introduce myself, just in case," I say carefully. "Maybe they wanted to confirm."

Auggie's silent as he digests my words. "Maybe," he says thoughtfully. "The records they accessed didn't confirm who you worked for. I actually thought you'd gotten a ticket or something, but I wanted to check to see if it was anything more."

"No. No infringement here—that I know of anyway. If it was a parking violation, they didn't leave a ticket."

"I'm sure it's nothing." His voice picks up, and I can almost hear the smile through his words. "I'll let you get back to your leave now. Thanks for information on those files. Chat later."

He signs off and leaves me wondering why anyone would run my name through the database. It wouldn't have been the sheriff; he's known who I am for months now. Even though he'd never met me in person before today, there'd be little to gain to conduct a basic police check. If he wanted to confirm my credentials, he would've gone straight to the bureau.

No, this is strange.

With the car in gear, I pull out onto the road, mind in overdrive. *What did Xander say?* Dawn was hanging around Jay and Conners in those last days of her visit here. Both of them are definitely on my short list. But Conners—a deputy sheriff according to my research— had the means to run the search. It's entirely possible he saw me in the sheriff's office and decided to do a bit of digging himself to identify who I was and what I was doing here. Small town and all, it's not that hard to find out most of that information. And the key hub for all information happens to be where I'm headed now.

TWELVE

Jamie Rogers.
Five-six.
Hazel eyes.
Home address: 7535 Lyncaster Road, Apartment #3.

THIRTEEN

Luke waves to me, and I follow the routine of my previous visits and take a seat in my booth. The diner is bustling with the lunch crowd, and the way everyone is carrying on leads me to believe that they're all locals. I study the interaction between some of the tables, recognizing faces.

Xander walks in, his open smile quickly disappearing when he sees me observing him. He sits down in the far corner booth with the petite, dark-haired woman, their heads bowed closely together as he whispers something to her. Her head jerks my way, eyes narrowing before Xander reaches for her hands across the table, directing her attention back to him. I can only imagine what he's saying to her and wonder how blown out of proportion it is or what slant is being told.

The clock is ticking.

It's going to be hard to hide my true intentions. I just hope the red herring of Xander's charging fiasco acts as a cover story long enough for me to run down my new leads. Even if most of the locals won't understand my questions and the deeper reasons for them, the killer will. He'll know very soon—if he doesn't already know—that I'm looking for him.

"Hey, do you mind if I sit here?" A man wearing work clothes and safety boots stands to the right of my table. "I wouldn't normally ask, but Luke suggested it'd be okay. He's trying to keep me and Sara-Lee apart, so it's probably best I don't sit at the counter. Or by myself." He shrugs as he talks and nods his head subtly toward the blonde sending daggers my way.

Before I can tell him it's not a good idea, Luke is by his side and gives him a little push toward the vacant seat across from me.

"Sorry, Jamie. Hope you don't mind." He hands me a menu. "Trust me, it's better for everyone if Jay sits here. I figured it'd be okay; he can answer almost any question you have about the area and brief you on all the best places to go."

Jay. Jayson?

One of the guys seen cozying up to the last victim. How coincidentally perfect.

Jay shoots me an apologetic look and slides into the booth.

"I'll be back to grab your order in a minute," Luke says after filling two cups with coffee.

Jay reaches his hand across the table. "Nice to meet you, Jamie. I'm Jayson Morris, but most people call me Jay."

Bingo.

Xander and his girlfriend give a knowing look, confirming that this Jay is his Jayson. What are the odds of one of my newly appointed suspects sitting across from me at lunch?

I smile, taking his hand. "Jamie Rogers. Temporary visitor, checking out the sights."

"Nice. Welcome, Jamie Rogers."

I look over his shoulder, noting the eyes on us. The whispering behind hands and knowing smirks prove too much for some. Sara-Lee huffs before standing, the ruffles of her skirt swaying with the motion, and she walks out without a backward glance. The reason for Jay sitting with me has gone, but I choose not to let him know, more interested in taking advantage of this opportunity to feel him out.

"So, what's the story with you and the girl?"

He cringes and barely holds himself still, trying hard to not look over in the direction of where he still believes Sara-Lee to be.

"As you've probably gathered," he says with a cheesy grin, "this is a small town. Everyone is always in your business. Well, me and SL dated back in school, and things ended amicably. But I went and wrecked that last year and hooked up with her after a drunken karaoke night."

I fail to see why this would have half the town gossiping and the other half refereeing between the two. There must be something more.

"And?" I prod gently.

His smile disappears, replaced with a contrite expression.

"And then I hooked up with her best friend the night after." He shrugs. "I didn't know she had been pining after me all these years and wanted something more. I would've steered clear if I had. Shit like that drags out so much here, and I screwed up royally."

I don't understand why something like that warrants such drama playing out between the two. Failed relationships justifying the theatrics. It's evident that everyone in the diner is aware and more than likely central to the reason this is continuing to remain in the limelight.

"Okay. What are you having?" Luke asks, pen at the ready.

Jay orders the burger with fries, and I follow suit.

"So, you've lived here all your life?" I ask Jay after Luke leaves to put our order in.

"Yes, ma'am. I worked at the resorts during summer, and after I left school, they took me on full-time, training me to do all the maintenance. It's not much, but it pays the bills."

Local boy, born and bred. I speculate if there's a reason he never thought to spread his wings and leave. Most young adults go off to college and live a bit before getting locked into the daily grind. I study him as he talks about the various resorts and what each of them offers in both the summer and winter months. He's animated and completely at ease. I'm just about to ask him about his family, wondering if they were somehow the catalyst for him never leaving, when Luke places our lunch in front of us. My question dies on my lips as I gorge myself on the juiciest burger I've ever eaten.

Our plates are almost clean when one of the uniformed deputies I remember seeing earlier this morning walks in to pick up lunch. Nothing about him looks out of the ordinary. His uniform is crisp and clean, and he holds himself proud, nodding to other patrons who happen to catch his eye. He freezes when he looks in my direction, the small smile playing on his lips morphing into a look of irritation. Jay turns to see what has taken my attention and groans.

"Friend of yours?" I ask, pondering their reaction to each other. Certainly not besties. "He looks as happy to see you as Sara-Lea was."

Jay laughs dryly. "Conners and I had a bit of a falling-out over a girl last month. He'll get over it."

Bingo.

And the girl last month would be Dawn Chapman. I can barely mask my excitement, able to covertly gather more information on my suspects. The deputy leaves, and Jay sighs in relief.

"Conners?" I ask, hoping he'll tell me more.

"Yeah, Deputy Sean Conners. He's divorced, if you're interested and stuffy and straitlaced are your type. Moved here a while back from the big city with a broken heart and has been looking for some nice girl to mend it ever since."

I ignore his comment, playing matchmaker. Conners is definitely not my type—unless it's his mug shot pinned on my suspect list. It's interesting he moved here so quickly after his divorce.

Is it the rejection of possible replacements that jaded him and prompted him to kill? Is that it? Could something like that turn a person into a killer?

My mind works overtime, playing out the various scenarios that would send Conners to become a serial killer. I have so many questions, but I'm not sure Jay is the one to answer them. Not without making him suspicious of my real agenda.

"Is it just me, Jay, or do you seem to have issues with most of the townsfolk?"

He chuckles. "It's just small-town politics. You learn to live with it."

I place money down to cover the cost of my lunch and push away from the table to stand. Jay follows suit and walks beside me, holding the door open for me to go through.

Jay seems like a nice guy. A bit of a womanizer to be sure, but he appears harmless. He didn't intimidate me at all, but he probably was on his best behavior, especially after being so openly outed with women issues. There were no negative or obscure vibes coming off him that screamed psycho or potential psycho. I need to follow up on his personal circumstances, why he was so content to stay here, forgoing college. But he seems dedicated to the community, if what he and others have said about him is true.

"I'm not sure where you're staying, but if it's at one of the hotels in town, you should come out to the tavern tonight. There's a band playing, and it should be fun."

I smile. "I'll think about it."

"That's all a guy can ask for." He heads over to the blue Dodge, jumps in, and turns the engine over. "See you later, Jamie Rogers."

I watch as he drives away in the direction of the town's resorts before turning around to walk to my vehicle. Parked on the corner about three cars back is a white Chevy, the driver sitting low behind the wheel. I would have missed him if I wasn't as observant and trained in counterintelligence measures to always be vigilant. It's Conners, and there's no mistaking the scowl on his face from watching Jay and me.

My first instinct is to go and confront him. Surely, there's a reason for him sitting there. But if he was the one to run my name through the police database, maybe I don't want to tip my hand just yet. I get in my car, deciding to ignore him and let things play out. This town isn't that big, and our paths will cross sooner rather than later.

Especially if he's the one I'm looking for.

FOURTEEN

You're curious.
I can see this.
Don't be, my love.

FIFTEEN

The cup of noodles doesn't taste even remotely as good as the food from the diner. I'm tempted to head out to the tavern to see the nightlife, grab a counter meal, and observe more of the locals interacting, but I decide not to. Loud music and drunken people are not my thing. Everyone more than likely knows who I am now and will have formulated their theories as to why I'm here. It's probably obvious it's not strictly for R&R.

I turn the TV to mute and close the blinds, shutting out the increasing dusk. It'll be dark soon, and although there's no reason for anyone to be out here, spying on me, I can't be sure. There were a few unsettling moments today when I felt eyes on me, and my senses are seldom wrong. I go through the bathroom and jimmy the locked spare room door and take a seat in front of my wall. I spent some time in here this afternoon, adding Post-it Notes, listing my suspects and everything I knew about them. I might or might not have logged on to my computer and run some checks of my own, but unlike the local sheriff's department, my searches are untraceable.

Xander Hays, twenty-seven years old. Single. He graduated from a local community college in a neighboring town. Unsurprisingly, Xander has a police record. It was sealed, misdemeanors from his youth.

Sean Conners, thirty-three years old. Divorced, no children. Graduate of the University of Tennessee. A handful of assault charges filed over the years a decade ago, but every single one of them was dropped the day after. These red flags didn't stop him from being admitted to the Knox County Sheriff's Office Regional Training Academy.

Jayson Morris, twenty-six years old. Single. Graduated with a high school diploma from Dark Hollow Lake Town High School. No felonies.

Xander admitted that Dawn had been involved with Conners and Jay. It might have been harmless fun. *But what if one of them wanted more?*

I lean back into the chair and close my eyes, replaying my interactions at lunch with Jay. I can't see this being the case with him; he didn't come across today as someone after commitment—just the opposite. He also clearly has a history with women in town, not just its visiting tourists. Surely, if he were unstable enough to demonstrate psychotic behavior against women, there'd be indications and undercurrents within the community.

Conners could have motive. He appears to have a history of mistreating women, the files I read telling a story of someone who probably shouldn't be in uniform. I don't care if the charges were dropped—where there's smoke, there has to be some sort of fire. One charge could be put down to a misunderstanding, but four ... unless the women he was dating at the time were manipulative attention-seekers. It's possible; I've seen cases like that before, and it could be why all charges were dropped.

Nothing's ever as black and white as it seems on paper or in front of you, unfortunately, but it's the aspect of my job I enjoy and excel at—to wade through those varying shades for the truth.

I run my hand through my hair and sigh. The truth is, although I made some headway today, I don't have enough information to know who the killer is. My gut, which is normally my guiding light, is uncharacteristically quiet right now. Which means my plan of becoming bait has to work. I'll need to draw the killer out and wait for him to trip up.

Glancing at the images to the left of my suspects list—the women who trusted the wrong guy and were punished for it—I know it won't take much. There's been too many now. He must want it out there, for people to know he's the one. That he's capable. He must be itching to take responsibility, so proud of his handiwork. We should be close to that point now of his evolution that it must be killing him that no one's aware all of these women are his.

Except for me.

SIXTEEN

Night-night, my sweet.

SEVENTEEN

Ratchet's Pass.

That's the goal today—to hike the trail up the pass to the scenic ridge line and then backtrack down past the waterfall to the rocked area where the pools are. I'm not expecting to find much, just to get an understanding of what the last victim was doing when that photo was taken. Trying to trace the last few days of her stay here in Dark Hollow Lake. I don't anticipate finding any clues, but going through these motions might be enough to spook the killer. Call it a hunch, but I'm betting my presence and actions will force him into showing his hand. And when he does, I'll be ready.

This thought exhilarates me, and my lips curl up into a smile. At Quantico, although I passed all of the field activities, my passion was always with the analytical side. During my training, I was dubbed the "savant of serials" with an uncanny ability to link together the most minute information within the case studies. Seeing the patterns no one else could see. Maybe this foray into the field is what I needed to break up the office-work monotony I hadn't even realized I was suffering from. That, and to prove my training title was no fluke.

I place the car in park and check the roughly drawn map, comparing it to what's meant to be the trailhead. It's missing the normal forestry sign and location map, but I easily make out the two timber posts on the cusp of the tree line that identifies the trail's starting point. It's unquestionably a locals-only known path, and I briefly contemplate how many tourists actually come this way. It's definitely off the beaten path.

With a few days spent in the area and up at the cabin, I've become accustomed to nature's symphony with its subtle nuances used to break up the silence. It's not as uncomfortable as it was the first morning I woke to it. The fresh air fills my lungs; it's invigorating.

My cell phone beeps, and I sigh at the incoming message, informing me of an upcoming sale at my favorite Washington boutique. I swipe and delete it, unread, only to watch as the one bar disappears and is replaced with the No Service tag. This is unexpected but not a problem. I'm confident with my physical abilities to conquer this trail safely, and Luke knows I'm here. My service Glock 19 is in my backpack with some trail mix and water, so it's not as though I'm defenseless. I take it out and strap on the front-body holster for easy access … just in case. It might be useless against a bear, but I'd rather have it out than not.

The path's narrow and mostly clear. So far, it's been distinguishable enough to guide me upward. Gleaming perspiration coats my arms and legs, pumping hard with the lungs working overtime to suck in the unfiltered forest air as I crest what I desperately hope is the final rise of the walk. Xander wasn't joking when he said it was a difficult hike. The vista unfolds before me. I take a seat on a chopped log, which must have been put here for that exact reason, and remove my water bottle. From this height, the town appears to be nothing more than speckled dots in the distance, attached to long, thin lines disappearing up the side of another mountain. A ravine separates my location to the ridge line connected with the resort's ski runs. Pity—otherwise, I might have hiked over to catch one of the chair lifts down.

The scenery's magnificent. I lean back and let the afternoon sun warm me. Not for the first time, a level of peace overwhelms me. It's hard at times like this to comprehend that a killer is walking free among all of this beauty and serenity. As though summoned by the thought of him, images of the last victim spoil the moment, and I reluctantly stand on a sigh. It's time to get moving. A quick scan of the area has me identifying the alternate path down that will return me to my car via the waterfall and rock pools.

The path heading down is narrower than the other one taken. The multiple cutbacks slow down the descent considerably, loose rocks and dirt slipping underfoot with each step. Rough bark scours my palms as I steady myself again after another short slide. It might be a shortcut down, but I see now why it's considered the more dangerous route and also why this trail's off the tourist map. I struggle to control my breathing and concentrate on my bearings, wishing not for the first time that I'd brought a trekking pole.

A loud crack sounds, and the forest seemingly goes silent. I remain motionless, trying to discern the sound and from which direction it originated. Seconds tick by, as though everything surrounding me holds its breath. Watching. Waiting. The small chatter of insects and birds start up, hesitantly at first before reaching the crescendo from the minutes prior. My hand that unconsciously gripped the stock of the pistol unclenches while I exhale slowly. The beauty I was admiring less than an hour ago now has an element of danger about it. Foreboding. Especially with me being out here alone.

I chuckle nervously, admonishing myself for freaking out with no good reason. The weight of the women murdered feels heavy today and especially present in this moment. I wonder if more than one of them walked this trail to see the pools and waterfall.

Did they do it alone, like me, or were they in the company of the killer?

These thoughts are the ones that worry me the most. From my brief observations of the townspeople in my fastidious attempt to identify the last victim's activities, only two names kept cropping up as potential suspects: Conners and possibly Xander. I haven't yet let go of Xander's reaction and the so-called banking error.

My mind plays over my interactions with them and what I know of their behavior, habits, and state of being. It could be either one of them, or it could be someone else completely. There are links missing, connecting each to all of the women I've identified. It is possible that there are two killers, but I find that highly unlikely. The deaths seemed to be personal and had an element of intimacy about them. The killer is smart in a lot of ways, but I honestly don't think he appreciates me being here and asking the questions that I have asked. It's only a matter of time before he shows his hand. I can feel it in my bones.

The waterfall comes into sight, and I'm happy to see it's running. Water gushes over rocks to its own melodic tune as light flickers happily between the movement. Taking a breather, I unscrew the lid to my water bottle to take a huge gulp and enjoy the spray from the falls that cools my body. Hair prickles on the back of my arms as a chill creeps down my spine. I slowly place the bottle back in my bag and adjust my cap, wiping the perspiration from my forehead while carefully studying my surroundings. I can't knock this feeling that something's not quite right. That there's someone or something watching me.

Slowly, I bend and once again don my backpack, determined to get to the rock pools as soon as possible. A quick glance at my cell confirms I'm still out of range for reception.

It takes another ten minutes before the ground levels out, and not only the rock pools, but also the lake come into view. I sigh with relief, thankful the last part of the hike is over. There's been a heaviness in the air ever since I started this descent, and it has all of my hackles raised and on alert.

I shake away these feelings of discomfort and concentrate on my immediate surroundings. My victim was here. Presumably with the killer … and his hairy, muscular leg and hiking boot. I take a few steps back, looking at the area in front of me and trying to work out where the image I saw was taken from. A flattened rock looks familiar, and I purse my lips, wondering whether she took the photos on a timer. If she did, then the camera could have been set up on the rock to my rear.

The angles definitely look right. Standing back, I'm convinced this is the location of those final images on Dawn's camera. Eyes closed, I try to imagine the scene play out.

She's happy. Laughing. Her companion making a joke or saying something that brings a smile to her face. They sit on one of the rocks and share some water and trail mix. Her camera is set up and placed on a timer to capture the memories. He leans over and puts his arm around her shoulders, whispering sweet words about how much he enjoys her company. She smiles shyly and leans in for a kiss, feeling relaxed and comfortable in his presence. He takes her camera and steps back to take some photos of her. They laugh again, and she places the camera on the rock and sets a timer to capture their moment.

I shake my head and take a deep breath before exhaling slowly. Cool mist rises from the silent pools, the surrounding green ferns swaying slightly. The stillness is absolute, chattering of the waterway I followed down from the falls gone silent. It's almost like my mind reenacting one of Dawn's final scenes in Dark Hollow Lake has cast a somber tone on the area. Too much time has passed for this to be a crime scene, any evidence long since washed away, but it doesn't stop me from going through the steps.

What if there was something left behind, connecting back to the killer?

But of course, there isn't.

I sit, and the cold seeps through my shorts. Frustrated with myself and the inability to find any clues, I empty the remaining contents of my water bottle. Rock scrapes my legs as I scoot closer to the edge of one of the pools. Small insects hover over the glass-like reflection, taunting the small fish darting to and fro. I watch their silver glimmer as they flash between their submerged hideouts.

My mind preoccupied with these somewhat-peaceful images and my own thoughts, I ignore a creeping darkness until a shadow separates me from the sun. I start to turn, feeling the presence behind me, but am unable to as a large black object hurtles in my direction. There's a loud smack, and stars explode before I fall into blackness.

Cold, hardened earth presses against the side of my body as I slowly regain consciousness. Breathing hurts. Each inhalation struggles through dry, parched lips before cold air rakes its way into my lungs. A dull, pounding pain pulsates near my temple, and my shaky hand reaches up to caress the location, only to meet a sticky heat.

My eyes adjust to the dappled light battling its way through the vegetation from the lowered sun. I push up slowly onto an elbow and fight the wave of nauseous dizziness. The sharp trill of a nearby bird explodes my nerves, and I instinctively move to grasp my handgun from my chest harness, only it's not there.

This is not right. Something is not right.

My backpack's lying a few feet to my right, zipped closed and propped against a rock. I don't remember putting it there. Small sticks and pebbles scrape the exposed skin of my legs as I awkwardly shuffle half-seated toward the canvas bag. Numb fingers struggle with the clasp, finally managing to pull it down. My belongings are all inside, including the Glock 19.

The smooth, hard metal provides a sense of security I didn't know I needed until I hold it in my hand. I stumble through the motions of checking the safety before expending the magazine to see the rounds. It clicks back in place in a single movement before I holster it.

I stand and slowly cast my eyes around, looking for any threat. Pain radiates from my head down to my legs, and I wince slightly, teetering in place. I need to get off this trail and back to my car before whoever or whatever did this to me comes back. Throbbing behind my eyes reminds me I need to get my head looked at as soon as possible. I'm sure I have a concussion, and I've no idea how far I am from the trailhead.

The sun is almost making its final descent when noise and movement ahead have me still, index finger now on the Glock's trigger. A short growl is the only warning I get before a large dog bounds out, and I squeal in surprise. My nerves are fried, and I wobble somewhat as my heart races. The motley Australian shepherd that sits a few feet from me, tongue lolling to the side of its open, panting mouth, has no idea how close he came to eating a bullet.

"Jamie? Oh my God. Jamie, are you okay?" Jay rushes up the path in my direction. His strong arms grasp mine as I lurch to the side, almost collapsing.

"I nearly shot your dog," I whisper, fumbling to clasp the gun back into its holster.

"Buster? No," he says, making light of what I said. "You'd never shoot him; he's too lovable."

Jay places his arm under mine and starts leading me down the trail. His next words hold a level of seriousness worlds apart from his previous ones. "What happened? How long have you been out here for?"

My mind works sluggishly through my options of what to tell him. He, like the whole town, knows I'm FBI, and I'm sure the rumor mill has sparked ideas about my covert reasons for being here. If I admit to him what I've been trying to achieve, will that help or hinder my investigation? He's a likable guy, but I don't know him. Although I don't think he could personally hurt a fly, he might be friends with the killer and say or do something that might tip him off. Tip him over the edge.

And the thing is, I don't really know what happened. Something that keeps going through my mind is that the killer was stalking me. Watching me. Playing with me. At this stage, I don't think I need to bring in any collateral damage by involving Jay with my theories of what happened and how.

"I fell," I mumble plainly. "Those switchbacks are not for the fainthearted."

"No," he agrees, stopping to look at me, "they're not. I know you're a tough special agent chick and all, but I wish I'd known you were coming out here. I could have accompanied you. There's a reason this trail isn't on the tourist list. It's dangerous."

Concern is etched in his eyes, and his lips purse slightly as his hand gingerly touches the cut above my eye. I wince at the contact and then at the redness on his fingers as he pulls back.

"The cut doesn't look bad, but there's a lump forming." He wipes his hand on his shorts and turns to lead me in the direction of the trailhead. "You'll probably have a nice bruise come up over the next few days."

Buster jogs off in front, stopping to sniff something off to the side every few minutes. He jingles as he moves, and I notice the bell dangling on his collar. I didn't notice the light ringing when he confronted me earlier.

"You're lucky we found you when we did. There've been reports of a bear in the area. You looking and smelling like a tasty human Popsicle could have attracted one. Another reason why you shouldn't be wandering around off the beaten track by yourself."

Of course there are bears. I am lucky Jay and Buster found me when they did.

My head clears, and I'm feeling less dizzy by the time we reach the cars. Jay's blue Dodge is backed in neatly next to mine on the gravel road. He helps me with my backpack and holds it for me while I search for the keys hiding in the bottom.

"Are you okay to drive?" he asks when I unlock and open the door. "I could drive you to the hospital if you want or follow you in my car. If you left yours here, we could come back tomorrow to pick it up."

I pause for a moment, exploring those options. I'm feeling much better physically; I don't even think I'll bother with going to the hospital or seeing a doctor. According to Jay's assessment, it's just a small cut, and I can easily patch that up back at the cabin with my first aid kit. I know what the doctor will say in regard to treating the concussion. I'd rather head straight to my cabin to relax, get my head around what really happened out here, and work out my next step. If I involve Jay, he'll be hanging around longer, and I just want to be by myself at the moment.

"No, I think I'm fine to drive. But thank you." I smile at his concerned expression and take the bag out of his hand, throwing it over onto the passenger seat. "I feel a bit foolish, falling and causing you concern. I just want to head back to my cabin and get some rest."

He's silent for a beat, studying my face. I don't move and hold my breath, waiting to see if he buys my nonchalant act.

"All right, if you say so." He pulls out a phone from his pocket. "Stop in at Luke's on your way. I'll call ahead and get him to prepare something for you."

I nod in response, wondering how he'll achieve that with no cellular network out here, and slide into the driver's seat. He hands me a worn business card, dog-eared in the corners, before I shut the door and lower the window.

"My cell is on there. In case you need something, call me."

"Thanks. And thanks for your help. Crossing paths with me when you did ..." My hands tighten on the steering wheel, and I quickly exhale. I turn and offer him a tight smile. "Thanks, Jay."

He nods and steps back, whistling for Buster to heel as I reverse the car, pointing it in the opposite direction. I watch his figure get smaller in the rearview mirror as I drive away. When I'm back on the main road, heading into town, my hands start to shake as my mind races.

What the fuck happened at the rock pools?

EIGHTEEN

Run, little rabbit.
    Run.
Scared little rabbit.
I have my rabbit's foot.
Smells divine.

NINETEEN

I'm still not sure what happened today. It's irking.

Deft movement makes quick work of finger-combing my hair, avoiding any pressure to the left side, near the contusion. Having been struck hard enough to lose consciousness, I admit, it doesn't look as bad as it should, which is lucky. *Glass half-full* type of lucky.

I leave the bathroom and relocate to the rocking chair on the porch, nursing a beer and ignoring the crispy aroma wafting from the fried chicken in Luke's takeout container on the small table beside me. I'm sure it's delicious, but at the moment, my stomach roils from my just thinking about it.

The heat of the day is fast disappearing, and the multitude of stars brighten the night sky. I awkwardly drag the scratchy afghan with one hand around my shoulders, pulling it tight to hold in the warmth of my recent shower. Silence is my companion, and I breathe it in, letting its calming waves envelop me.

The facts.

I run the facts, what I know and what I don't know, mentally checking them off one at a time.

I know an animal is incapable of sneaking up on a person to render them unconscious and frisk through their belongings.

I know it wasn't a bear.

I don't know if it was premeditated or opportunistic.

I know that the attack didn't have any trademarks of the killer.

I don't know if the attacker intended to return.

I don't know if my regaining consciousness foiled something else, something more sinister.

The warm beer loses its crispness and sours in my mouth. I leave it on the table next to the food and go back inside, pulling the patchwork throw tighter around me. Exhaustion sways me into the doorframe of the bedroom, and I hold out a hand to steady myself. The pulse on my temple throbs slowly, and I find myself again in front of the mirror, checking the bruise's progression.

It's there. It hasn't gone away.

I slowly run my fingers through my hair, and for the first time, I notice the unevenness in its length as the now-dried locks fall freely around my face.

What the fuck?

It's like a swarm of bees are suddenly buzzing, drowning out all noise of reality. My knees weaken, and I fall toward the mirror, hips connecting harshly with the top of the stone bench. Mouth agape, I watch the reflection of me pulling the strands over my ears. There's over two inches of hair missing, the ends of the shorn pieces jagged from small, uneven, angled cuts.

Someone cut my hair. While I was lying unconscious, facedown in the dirt, someone cut my hair, taking it like some perverted trophy.

This is fucked up.

I blink, suddenly wide awake. *Have I missed something, or has the killer been leaving me clues this whole time?*

Moving into my secret sanctuary, I open the case files, poring over the reports, searching between the lines for indications of any unreported mementos. It's not uncommon for a killer to keep something to connect them with the crime, something that tethers the two of them. Something he can see or touch to prolong the fantasy of the crime, relive it. Nothing materializes as missing, assuring me that I didn't overlook anything the first time. With the help of a magnifying glass and the reading lamp, I study the scene photos, paying particular attention to the friction burns around the victim's wrists and neck. Skin slowly abraded by a tight, coarse rope, the areas are red and angry. Again, I find nothing.

Has he switched up his MO or …

Or was he alerting me to the fact that he knows what I'm up to?

How dangerous is this guy?

I know he kills, but that's only after he pulls his victims into his web of seduction and they let their defenses down. They don't know what he is or what he wants from them. They don't expect him to carry out such an act of perverse violence when they look away. I, however, do.

Is he capable of exacting something more violent and more aggressive against someone who knows what he is?

I don't know, and it doesn't matter because in this game of cat and mouse, I am going to come out the victor.

Having penned my main question on the yellow Post-it, I stick it on my wall, next to my possible suspects. My fingers grasp the note with Jay's name and slowly peel it off. After today, I'm less sure Jay deserves to be on that list.

My hand sweeps my hair behind an ear in a habitual movement, stopping to again rub the newly cut section.

Tomorrow. I'll get my answers tomorrow.

TWENTY

Surprise.
Yes, you are … special.

TWENTY-ONE

It's early, but I know he'll be in. I've decided to report the incident at Ratchet's Pass to the sheriff. Although I'd prefer for nothing to be recorded formally, he does need to be aware of what happened. I'll also take the opportunity to pick his brain about some of my possible suspects based off town gossip and observations. Hard evidence is what's needed to convict a killer, but sifting through all the hearsay and rumors is what's done to catch a killer. Intuition plays an important role during investigations, and sometimes, it's the smallest of things that seem off for no reason that develop into red flags for me.

The front door is open; however, the desk clerk is absent. I'm about to push the after-hours service bell when Sheriff Layton appears past the partition, coffee in one hand and a pastry in the other.

"Jamie?" he says, surprised, lowering his drink from his lips.

"Sheriff, I was hoping to have a quick word."

"Sure. Come on through." He places the coffee on the counter for the few seconds it takes to disengage the door. "You'll have to excuse me while I eat my breakfast."

I adjust the Cubs cap on my head and follow him through to his office.

"I heard you had a nasty fall yesterday out on Ratchet's Pass," he says, taking a seat behind his desk. "I caught up with Jay this morning. He was worried it could have been a bad concussion. But I figured everything was okay since you hadn't checked in at the hospital."

He places his pastry down on top of a pile of files, glancing down at it longingly before sitting back and providing me with his full attention.

"Yes. That's one of the things I wanted to discuss. My accident wasn't an accident." I pause a moment, gauging his reaction before continuing, "I was struck from behind, and while I was knocked unconscious, someone cut my hair."

"Say what now?"

Removing the cap, I pull my hair free from its ponytail and shake it out. He leans over the desk, peering at the part angled toward him. With some of the unevenly short pieces pinned between two fingers, I hold them up as proof.

"Well, shit." Eyebrows furrowed, he shakes his head. "And how exactly did this come about?"

I quickly twist my hair back under the cap and retell the events of yesterday, explaining my need to follow in the last victim's footsteps as close as possible and the sense I got out there of being watched. He listens, asking for clarification every now and again.

"And that's when Jay and Buster found you," he says, finishing my story.

"Yes," I say, nodding slowly. "And I find the timing of that strange. His name keeps popping up everywhere I go. I can't work out if he should be number one on my suspect list or not at all."

The sheriff taps his fingers on his lips, as though in thought, while a slow smile builds on his face. "I can see why you'd think that. Jay's a good guy. He's misunderstood by a lot of people around town due to his penchant to indiscriminately hook up with any pretty young thing. I wouldn't be surprised if he doesn't try to sweet-talk you too." The finger wagged in my direction is accompanied by a short, dry laugh.

The sheriff's ears redden as he realizes his words, unable to take them back. The mirth disappears as suddenly as it came, replaced again with the no-nonsense professional.

"I like Jay. I've known him practically his whole life. He is a bit of a legend around here. Did you know he's a volunteer firefighter? A few years back, he pulled ol' widow Milly from her burning home and then went back to free her animals from the flaming barn before it exploded."

The sheriff goes quiet, his gaze becoming distant. I want so desperately to probe, needing to understand more and add to the building profile in my mind, but his expression stills my tongue.

"The fires that year near on threatened the whole town," he says quietly with a grim twist of the mouth. "Marty—that's the fire chief—relies heavily on the volunteers to do what he does. Jay's one of the best. He's always there, ready to go when needed."

I shake my head, trying to consolidate my image of Jay and the one now being painted by the sheriff.

"He had it tough, growing up, losing his father early on and his mom struggling with alcohol abuse. But he never let his family circumstances pull him down. He was a good kid—and still is." Sheriff Layton hesitates before continuing, weighing his words carefully, "He might come across as the jokester, but he's a hard worker and loyal. He's one to be relied upon. I can't see him being capable of hurting anyone."

I study the sheriff as he fidgets with a pen on his desk. He's been working in Dark Hollow Lake for over a decade. Ample enough time to observe a lot of its residents, like Jay, growing up.

But how well does he know his staff?

"How long has Deputy Conners worked here?"

The sheriff's eyes meet mine, head flinching back slightly. "I'm sorry, what?"

"Conners," I repeat. "How long has he been in Dark Hollow Lake?"

"Huh," he says, tugging on his ear. "He transferred in three years ago. Why?"

"No reason. I ran a check on some names that popped up and saw the assault allegations made against him."

The sheriff breaks eye contact and takes a deep breath, exhaling against the fist now tapping against his lips.

"I know about those—knew before he transferred in." He looks up and sighs at the expression he must see on my face. Reluctantly, he continues, "I don't want you digging into his affairs, so I'll tell you what I know. From what I understand, he married his high school sweetheart, and she went off the rails. Drugs. Ended up involved with some criminal element. He tried for a few years to get her on the straight and narrow, rehab and the like, but it didn't work. She chose the drugs. His divorce was messy, as you can imagine, and he decided on starting over somewhere new."

He meets my eyes, a hard glint forming behind the glare. "This isn't common knowledge, and I don't want it out there," he says, gesturing outside with his hand. "I believe in second chances and hope he finds it here. Sean Conners can be a bit brash, but he's a good deputy."

I nod, thankful the goodwill he feels toward me has allowed him to share as much as he has.

"Well, Sheriff, I really wanted to come in to let you know where I was at with my inquiries." I absently push back the pieces of hair that have fallen from under the cap. "And informally report my attack."

He starts to speak, but I cut him off, "If you can, give me a day or two … so I can see what comes of it. I promise, before I leave, I'll file a formal report."

Pursed lips suggest he's not happy about any of this, but his resigned sigh is all I need to know I've been given a temporary reprieve. "Okay. But make sure you do."

I offer him a tight smile and make my exit to think over this new information and strategize over a new plan.

TWENTY-TWO

"C'mon, it'll be fun."

I'm in the diner, huddled in a corner booth, nursing a coffee. An oversize sweater hides my hands with the sleeves pulled over them. I've attempted to camouflage the bruising on my face with the Cubs cap, tugging the brim low to make it difficult for anyone to see my eyes. As I slouch in old, comfortable clothing, it's like the diner has become an extension of my home. I hoped people wouldn't notice me and that I could hole up and people-watch for the day while I considered my next move.

But of course, that was too much to ask.

"It's probably going to be the last one for the season. You survived Ratchet's Pass; you're pretty much a local now. So, you have to come."

"Stop hassling my patrons, Jay. Don't make me put another ban on you," Luke says half-jokingly. He tops off my coffee and leaves a plated piece of key lime pie.

"Okay, I'm sorry," Jay says on a sigh. "Listen, the offers still stands. There's a small patch of beach to the east of the dive shop on this side of Sevier Bridge. You can follow the path pretty much all the way down. You won't miss it. It'll be chill. Hope to see you there."

I nod noncommittally, pulling the pie closer. Jay stands and leaves with a small wave just as the door to the diner opens and Deputy Conners enters. His entrance sucks all of the air from the diner, the rapidly falling pressure noticeable as everyone seems to hold their breath at the same time. The other day when he was in, I didn't notice the effect he had on people; I only observed the disdain he showed toward Jay.

What did the sheriff call him … brash?

The disdain is mutual, going by Jay's straightening posture as the two pass each other. Jay pushes the door open and half-turns back, a frown on his face. I ponder if the real reason for the dislike is an abhorrence to authority or if there's something more. The vibe between the two appears more than a superfluous tiff over a female tourist.

Conners's mask is unreadable when Luke calls out to tell him his order isn't ready yet. He nods and turns toward my booth.

"Special Agent Jamie Rogers," he says neutrally, sitting down opposite me, uninvited.

The cold metal prongs of the fork lightly scrape my teeth as I slowly remove it from my mouth, placing it neatly next to the half-eaten pie. His eyebrows lift, partially questioning but mostly as a challenge.

"Deputy Sean Conners."

If he's surprised by me knowing his name, he doesn't show it. I sit back, crossing my arms in front of my body, and wait to see what he wants.

"How's your 'vacation' been going?" His lips curl slightly into a quick sneer as he makes little air quotation marks on the word *vacation*.

"Good, thank you." I'm not sure what's promoted such a hostile visit, but two can play this game. It's not uncommon for the local authorities to feel threatened if the FBI invade their turf.

Da-dum. His index and middle fingers tap a rhythmic beat against the table. *Da-dum, da-dum, da-dum*. They're stubby with yellowing nails, chewed to the quick. The tapping of the pads is forceful enough to vibrate through the retro laminate.

"What are you really doing here, Special Agent?" he asks, pulling my attention from his hand to his face. "It's not for recreation. You haven't done anything at all remotely touristy since you arrived. And if your intent was to switch off and relax, you'd be spending more time doing that and less time walking around town, questioning townsfolk."

I pause briefly to mull over his words. This comment highlights three things for me: it lets me know that the sheriff hasn't seen fit to brief his staff, I've done a terrible job of hiding my true intent for being here, and I've piqued his interest enough for him to confront me. I also get this feeling he doesn't like not knowing; it irks him.

"I don't know what you're talking about, Deputy."

The drumming on the table continues as the corners of his mouth pull up into a derisive smile. It matches the piercing eyes that have yet to break contact with mine. I'm itching to fidget, to nervously tug on the shorn bits of hair. Thoughts from yesterday, wondering how long I was lying cold and unconscious on the ground after being struck by someone, flood back. The trinket someone took from me while I was in that state. While I struggle to remain still, I scrutinize my potential suspect in detail.

"You're up to something, and I don't like it. And you know what?" The tapping ceases and he sits back, crossing his arms, mirroring my pose. "I don't think you're authorized to be here."

Interesting conclusion.

"Let me ask you something, Deputy. Do you normally keep such close tabs on all the tourists? Or just the ones who seem to be, in your opinion, acting against the norm?"

He shakes off my insult and straightens his posture. Darkness bleeds into his eyes while his nostrils flare. Arms twitch somewhat, slightly drawing my attention to clenched fists with whitening knuckles. I find it telling that my question triggered this response.

"You don't like Jay much, do you?"

"Do you?"

"I have no idea. I know him about as well as I know you." I shrug noncommittally before leaning forward, my hands holding the edge of the table, and say softly, "As well as you also knew Dawn."

He remains completely calm, and I watch as his pupils constrict back to normal. He exhales, rolls his head to the side, and cracks his neck.

"You're here because of Dawn Chapman? She was here last month."

He studies me, and I blink slowly under the increasingly uncomfortable scrutiny while watching him for any telltale give. Waiting for him to do or say something that might incriminate him or someone else. It's a dangerous intellectual game of predator and prey.

"I know," I say to trap him.

"That payment issue was sorted." The lilt in his voice is questioning, as if he's uncertain of what I know and what I don't know. The rapping on the tabletop resumes.

"That I also know."

"Hey, Conners. Your food's ready," Luke calls out from behind the counter, holding up a takeout bag.

Conners gives him a nod and pushes away from the table to stand. Before stepping away, he bends to say something just quiet enough for me to hear. "Don't go to the bonfire. You don't belong here."

I watch as he pays for his meal and exits the diner. He and Jay are polar opposites, and I have no idea what Dawn was doing if she was leading them both on. Jay is definitely a womanizer but a decent guy at the core. But Conners just seems to not like women, judging by this interaction and what I know so far from my due diligence.

"What was going on there?" Luke asks, topping off my coffee. "Conners is normally weird, but that was strange, even for him."

I shake my head. I don't know. I really don't know.

"What's the big deal about this bonfire?" I ask, changing the topic and asking the question that's been on my mind since Jay mentioned it. "I would've thought parties like that were more a high school senior thing."

Luke smiles. "Yeah, I could see how you might think that. But there're some legends that date back to the eighteenth century. This end-of-season bonfire is meant to bring good luck and prosperity to those that attend. It's like some witchy ceremony, or the like, without all that hocus-pocus stuff. Some folks believe all that supernatural mumbo jumbo; others just like to go hang out by the lake under the stars."

My mouth drops open, and I'm at a loss for words. I read some of the lore and mystery about Dark Hollow Lake but figured it was there to pull the tourists in, get them exploring ruins and caves. I never once thought the locals actually bought into any of it.

"Seriously, Jamie, it's just a bonfire. People hanging out, sharing some 'shine by the lake. The only spirits there will be the one in the moonshine bottles."

He walks away, and I'm left speechless. I'm way too old for a college-style party by the lake, but from what Luke just shared, I'm tempted to go and see how it differs. Weirdos indeed. It's probably another tourist trap, upping the intrigue to get a higher attendance. When Jay asked, I had no intention to go, but now, my interest is piqued.

The bonfire is also one of the events Dawn attended during her stay at Dark Hollow Lake. There wasn't any photographic evidence on her camera that I found, but if what Xander said was true, both Jay and Conners were vying for her attention that night. Just like in their own ways, they both asked me to attend tonight. Coincidence? I'm not sure.

I leave some cash on under my empty plate and walk to the counter. "Hey, Luke. Where's the best place to buy some moonshine?"

TWENTY-THREE

You should come.
You will come.
But maybe you shouldn't.

TWENTY-FOUR

I'm trying to think about how much I've been following Dawn's footsteps, both by accident and design. It's an easy path to follow even if I didn't have the intent to do so.

Did all of the five other women do the same?

Did each of them follow this darkened walkway with the promise of a party?

A step away from the norm of the tavern and its local bands, bingo, or karaoke. It's weird, but only after a few short days, this town has a level of familiarity about it. I don't feel as though I am the same person who walks through the doors of the bureau every day to run the names and numbers to help bring people to justice. I've taken the pantsuit off, and everything I know has been thrown out the window.

What am I doing?

I'm acting more like some amateur Nancy Drew from a poorly rated mystery series rather than a highly trained FBI agent. I came to this town to find answers … unofficially. I know that there's only so much I can do unofficially. But I shouldn't be intimidated by anyone in this town. The killer wants to fuck with me? Bring it. I will not let him or anyone get the jump on me again. What happened out on that trail was fucked up, but it shows I am on the right path. I think I'll rattle him enough, so he says or does something, and it doesn't have to be much. I know him. I've read the files. I know him probably better than he knows himself. He can't help himself … he has to react. Me being here must have him chomping at the bit. Ruffling his feathers.

Bring it.

The smooth timber railing is cold beneath my hand. I've come to the end of the path, and there's a handful of rock-lined steps to walk down to the lakeside. Firelight illuminates the area, providing an ethereal ambience, as small groups of people congregate on the sandy shore.

It's not hard to make out the people I've seen around town, armed with drinks. Their laughter is music, wafting with innocence and shrouding the killer among them. Unaware of the wolf lurking in the shadows, they dance and talk while toasting the freedom of their lives.

All, except one.

Conners sits alone to the side. Not completely out of the circle of light, but not quite in it either. A six-pack of beer rests next to his feet. He watches, silent and motionless as a statue, the only movement being his arm dragging the bottle to his mouth.

Protector or predator?

The questions churn through my mind. *Is he the one? Does he kill the women who spurned him? Those who choose others over him, thus making him look a fool? Just like his wife chose drugs? Did he let his past relationship define who he is and dictate his future ones?*

Footsteps from the path draw my attention away from the beach. The partial darkness makes it difficult to make out who's there until they're almost upon me. Xander and the pixie-like brunette from the diner—Rory, the former archeologist, now town librarian and girlfriend to Xander if my eavesdropping is correct. His feet shuffle to a standstill, and his smile disappears when he realizes it's me standing here.

"Special Agent Rogers. Didn't expect to see you here."

I shrug, not knowing how to answer Xander's unspoken question of why I'm here. It's not as though I'd tell him the truth—that it's because one of my suspects asked me to come and another told me to stay away. I haven't forgotten his strange behavior in his store.

As though hearing my thoughts, Rory narrows her eyes, and she creeps an arm around Xander's waist, offering unvoiced strength and support. She tugs on his shirt, and like a puppet, he reacts.

"Oh, have a good evening then."

They hurry off down the steps and join the others already on the beach, exchanging pleasantries as they go. I turn my attention back to Conners, surprised to see him looking my way. He raises the hand holding the glass bottle in a salute my way before upending its contents.

Walking down the steps, I cautiously approach the gathering, noting the looks and whispers directed toward me. Again, I remind myself why I'm here—because of Dawn and the other women. The taste of smoke gets stronger as I approach the firepit closest to Conners.

"You're a brave one; I'll give you that. Or stupid." He shrugs, mocking me with his actions.

I glance around briefly, clutching my bag closer to my midriff. No one else seems to have heard his words.

"I honestly don't know what your problem is," I respond, the lie coating my tongue.

Conners's mouth pinches, and he lifts his chin in contempt. He looks as though he's about to say something else, but he clenches his jaw and looks away just as I'm grabbed from behind.

My squeal is barely audible as my muscles freeze up, and I drop the bottle of moonshine as I'm spun around one hundred eighty degrees.

Jay.

Nervous laughter bubbles out, tension from a moment ago broken.

"You made it. I knew you would and just in time." He bends over and dusts the sand off my alcohol before dragging me over to a group of people getting comfortable around an acoustic guitarist. "This guy's great. Hang here for a minute. I'll chase down a cup for your drink."

He races off to another group, leaving me among strangers. I smile tightly and focus my attention on the dreadlocks of the performer. He flicks them over his shoulder and casually starts strumming a popular tune with a fluorescent-green pick, movements appearing like busy off-color fireflies.

"Here you go." Jay reappears and holds out a reminder of my college years in the guise of a red plastic cup. "Sit down. Enjoy yourself."

The dampness of the sand soaks through my jeans and acts as a coolant to the heat of the nearby flames. My cup is filled, and Jay places the now-half-empty bottle of moonshine at my feet. Taking a sip, I purse my lips in disgust at the strong, bitter taste of liquor. When I chose the moonshine, it was at random. More of an impetuous buy than anything. I didn't think I'd need anything to mix it with, and I regret not just bringing my whiskey.

I take another sip and force a smile as Jay flits off to another group of people. The drink's pungent, and I set it down next to the bottle, enjoying the moment to unobtrusively watch the interactions between everyone and eavesdrop on discussions I can make out over the music.

"I know you've seen Dawn. That you know. You should watch yourself."

My body stiffens, heartbeat thundering in my ears. His breath in my ear is warm and wet. I shudder and turn in time to see him disappear into the shadows. The only reminder that he was actually here is the stench of fermented barley lingering around my face.

Was that a threat?

I grimace and reach for my drink, taking a mouthful and swallowing before being reminded of its own repulsiveness. Spluttering, I push it away and watch it tip. The vile liquid sinks into the sand until it disappears.

What is Conners's endgame?

My body's strumming with unfamiliar energy. Ever vigilant, I process everyone around me. Again, his actions went unnoticed, like he's a ghost. He confound me.

Slowly, my nerves calm. Any thoughts of following Conners leaves my mind as I become super aware of my heightened surroundings.

The fire ...

The chatter …
The cool breeze blowing across my face …
The grit of the sand in my socks …
The green fireflies riding the musical notes …

Nameless faces dance around in the shadows, moving with the music. My body joins in, swaying softly in place.

"Hey—Jamie, are you okay?"

Whiskey, not beer. His face has blurred edges.

I raise my hands to cup them around my cheeks. They're hot, owing to the neighboring flames … and the alcohol. I right the cup, bringing it to my nose and inhale. Jay gently takes it from my hand.

"Moonshine can be very potent. Especially on an empty stomach." Sparks flicker behind him, illuminating his concern. "Have you eaten since lunch?"

It's as though my head has the weight of a bowling ball as it moves from side to side, signaling a no. I hardly ate all day. Plenty of coffee, not much food.

"C'mon. Let's get you out of here. I'm sure you don't want anyone seeing you like this."

Jay pulls me up and places an arm around my waist, taking most of my weight. With care, he directs me away from the beach hideaway and along the path to the parking lot. Away from the heat of the fires, my body temperature rapidly causes me to shiver.

"I can drop you off at Bobby's cabin and organize for someone to drop your car off in the morning, if you'd like."

I nod as he assists me into the truck and straps me in. It sounds like a plan. The rumble of the engine vibrates, rocking me toward slumber. Hot air from the vents warms me. Before I succumb to sleep, I wonder

what Conners put in my drink to send me over the edge
this quickly.

TWENTY-FIVE

I open the door wide and inhale. It smells like her. She's only occupied the space for a handful of days, and already, her scent permeates through.

This isn't how I wanted our experience to be. I was hoping to go back to Washington and visit her in her home, get to know her better. But it's probably better this way. She's getting close to figuring it out—I can see it in the way she looks at me. And although my name's been moved down on her shrine to me, it's still there.

The shrine.

Well, well, well … that was a pleasant surprise. I'd thought my tributes had gone unnoticed. That they were secrets, just mine. It wasn't until recently that I realized how much I wanted people to see me. To see what I was capable of. But she saw me.

She *sees* me.

In every body she studies, dissects with her mind, she sees me.

She looked beyond the skin of the magnificent masterpieces and acknowledged the work that had gone into them. That I am more. More than my existence in this dark hellhole.

A woman like Jamie deserves to know she's special ... and she'll know soon enough.

The cushioned timber chair in the corner, sporting sturdy arms, catches my eye. I take my time to center it in the room and drop the ropes beside it. It's perfect.

Now, for the *pièce de résistance* ... and she's going to be brilliant.

Gravel crunches underfoot as I rush back to the car. There's movement in the front seat. What the— she shouldn't be conscious just yet. She mustn't have drunk the entire dose, the empty cup a lie.

"Ja-mieeeee," I singsong, approaching the passenger window. "Ja-mieeeee ... whatcha doing?"

I laugh, hand on the door handle, readying to pull it open. At least I had the foresight to bind her hands after she fell asleep. With her hands tied, there's not too much she can do. Legs connect with my midsection, forcing me back a few steps and stealing my breath. Her body flops out of the truck cabin, the drug affecting her coordination. She lands on her knees, and I relish the opportunity to kick her down. She slams into the ground face-first with a grunt.

"What are you doing, Ja-mieeeee? Think you can get away, Ja-mieeeee?"

"F-f-fuuuck you!"

Her whimpered reply brings a smile to my face.

This is going to be fun.

I drag her up by the collar of her jacket, forcing her to stand. Under my direction, we stumble-walk inside, her bravado short-lived. It's easy work to seat and secure her in the chair.

From previous visits, I know there's an open bottle of whiskey in her luggage. I retrieve it, pulling the stopper out and taking a long pull. I wasn't sure if she'd turn up at the bonfire tonight. I hoped. Waiting, I drank one or three too many beers. Not enough to be drunk—never drunk—just enough for a good buzz. The whiskey adds to that, my head quieting for a blissful moment.

Her eyes follow my movements as I return from the bedroom and settle into one of the sofas. Slack, deteriorating springs show their age, and I sink down low. *Bobby really needs to upgrade the furniture in here.*

"Why are you doing this?" Her words slur, tongue too heavy from the little Rohypnol she consumed.

I shrug. "I think you know why. I can't let you expose me."

And I can't. As much as I want to be seen, I don't want to be caught. I don't know what evidence I left behind at the crime scenes for her to come sniffing around, but I need to find out. Life's too short— something my girls can attest to—and I'm having too much fun to just up and quit now. Or get locked away.

She mumbles something incoherent, but I ignore her, pulling my cell phone from my pocket to check on the time. It's unfortunate that tonight will be hurried, but I need to leave within the hour to ensure I'm cleared of suspicion.

I'll need an alibi. My mind goes to Sara-Lee, and I smile, tapping a message to her. Sara-Lee won't be able to resist, and the follow-on drama from our hook-up will keep the gossipers in check. Other than confirming I dropped her drunk ass off at Bobby's cabin, no one will question me about the demise of FBI Special Agent Jamie Rogers.

Message sent, alibi coordinated, I move my attention back to the task at hand. This time round will be rushed, and it's a pity. We haven't even been intimately acquainted. I check the time again and pout because we won't be. Jamie's button-up is low enough for me to make out the contours of treasures underneath, but they're not mine. Not this time. And I doubt they would have ever been.

No. It's probably best to end this threat and move on. The fallout will be tough. I'll have to become more creative to find new playthings that won't link back to me.

"You've spoiled all of my fun, Jamie. Why would you come here, asking questions, trying to flush me out?" I crouch in front of her and take a swig. "I mean, I'm super impressed you found me. And I'm flattered you thought enough of me to come looking. But there's something I need to know. I need to know what it was that had you connect the girls."

Bloodshot eyes blink heavily at me, but I can see the intelligence behind them. She can understand me. Her mind might be working overtime, dragging slowly, as though through mud, but it's there. She's there. She will answer me.

I continue talking, waiting for her mouth to catch up, "You know, you missed a few … but they were my first. I hadn't established my methods then. Hadn't refined them. But I was careful."

Moving behind her, I run my fingers through her hair. It's soft with the texture of finely spun silk. She washed it tonight before going out, the undertone of fruit subtly fragranced beneath the smokiness from the bonfires.

Bringing my mouth down toward an ear, I whisper, "So, how, Jamie? How?"

My words have barely left my mouth when her head strikes out, connecting with my face.

"Ow! Fucking bitch!"

The blood drips down my face, and I pinch my nose to lessen the flow. Her chuckle is deep and cadenced, like a slow clap from an audience of one. I see red, and before I can stop myself, I'm in front of her, relishing the matching drip from the corner of her mouth after it had the misfortune to connect with my backhand.

"Why?" Her eyes meet mine. "Why did you kill all those women? I figured out the connection, but I couldn't figure out the why."

"Women like you will never understand. You think you know it all. Deserve it all. But you don't."

The kitchen has a roll of paper towels, and I pull a few sheets to clean up my blood. A few drops landed on the floor, and I don't need to leave any traces of DNA here for the authorities to identify me. Opening the cupboard under the sink, I grab the all-purpose cleaner. It'll have to do. I peer over the counter at a scraping sound and see Jamie trying to move the chair closer to the coffee table, and I laugh.

"See! Even now, you think you can best me, are better than me," I say, moving back in front of her. "I'm so sick of those who come here, thinking they're so good. So much better than us, me. Flashing your wealth around town, partying with us, leading us on."

Spittle flies from my mouth as my ire rises. The bloody napkin forgotten, I place my hands on my head, pacing in front of her restrained body. "Then, you leave. I was sick of it. I wanted more. But they never did." I come to a standstill in front of her for our eyes to lock. "So, they paid for it."

"That doesn't make any sense," she says calmly. "You killed the women because they had a holiday fling in the tourist town you live and work in?"

I pull at my hair. Of course she wouldn't understand. She wouldn't know what it's like to grow up poor and unwanted. With an abusive alcoholic who spent all her time resenting me. Blaming me for my father's death …

"You know she killed him. Yep, she made it look like an overdose, and technically, it probably was, but she was the one who pushed the plunger into the barrel of the syringe. She was the one who did it."

The sofa creaks as I sit. Remembering those days … that day is filling my head with ardor I can't ignore. It's the catalyst for all the highs I've gotten since putting those stuck-up bitches out of their misery once they tried to move on. From me …

"I always looked after her even though she made it difficult. Maybe I looked too much like him, reminded her of him. I don't know, but she told me one day what she did. Admitted it. I grew up without a father because of her selfishness."

I look over toward Jamie; the blood around her mouth has dried. She's a looker for sure, way out of my league. There'd be no future with her, not that I'd want one. I need to end this now, the way I ended my mother all those years ago.

Selfish bitches need to pay.

The pillow is firm but light in my hands. It'll work to restrict her breathing, and if I hold it just right, I'll be able to see the spark of life dissolve to nothing in her eyes. I can work out how to stage it later, to make it look accidental.

TWENTY-SIX

"**P**ut … hands where … see 'em."

All sounds blend together.

My eyelids slowly peel open. They're weighted down and not responding to muddled thought commands. All I know is that my life will end soon, at the hands of Jay. Hopefully, my death will be the last for him; he surely won't be able to cover this up.

Bright lights pierce my corneas, momentarily blinding me. Blotched vision obstructs my view of blackened blobs moving …

Blurred images fuss around me, and I flinch when something … someone touches me.

Has the cavalry arrived?

I can't make them out. But there's more than just Jay here now.

That has to be good?

" … okay …"

I know that voice.

I think.

The sheriff? Is that Conners as well?

TWENTY-SEVEN

I'm in a hospital bed.

The room is bright and cheery with yellow daisies in a small glass on the bedside table. My body's stiff, and my head throbs as I try to move. A light dressing wraps my wrists, protecting the rope burns.

Birdsong makes its way through the closed window, and I watch as the small sparrows play chase on the air currents while trying to remember the circumstances that brought me here.

The murders. Dark Hollow Lake. The bonfire.

Jay.

"You're lucky."

I startle at the words and twist slowly to see Conners sitting in a chair in the corner of the room, almost as though he didn't want to be seen.

"I tried to warn you." He stands and moves to the side of the bed, hat in hand. "I told you to stay away from the lake. From the bonfire."

My eyes close, the dull pounding behind my temples increasing, and I remember our discussion at the diner and the bonfire and how certain I was that there was something off about it all. Something that didn't quite add up.

"Did you know?" The words are whispered, and I open my eyes, searching for some water or ice to relieve the dryness of my throat.

Conners fidgets before reaching over to pour water from the plastic beige decanter on the table beside me. I gratefully take the offered cup, and with shaky hands, I lift it to my mouth.

"I wasn't sure what I knew," he offers. "There's been some sketchy behavior going on in these parts for a while now. I didn't piece it together until you came, asking questions and stirring the locals up."

My brows furrow, and I shake my head slightly in disagreement, wincing at the pain. "I didn't stir anyone up; my questions were subtle."

Conners sighs. "Whether you intended to or not, you stirred shit up," he says, tapping his stubby fingers on his uniform pants. "I had my suspicions once I read the file on Ms. Chapman. But I wasn't sure until a BOLO was issued and … we found you."

I nod. It makes sense. Sort of. I'm sure it will when the headache dissipates and I can think clearly.

"Jay's one nasty SOB; that's for sure." His words trail off, and I close my eyes, not bothering to fight the sleep calling me.

Footsteps echo outside my door, and my head moves in time to see the handle turn. Auggie peers through the crack, only to smile and push it open and make his way to the side of my bed. He places a paper coffee cup on the tray and nudges it in my direction.

The silence continues until after he takes a sip of his coffee and sits. "I heard they have shit coffee here, so I grabbed one to go from the local diner."

"Luke's?" I ask, voice raspy, participating in the mandatory small talk.

"Yeah."

My hand shakes, lifting the coffee to my lips. The heat burns the cut on the side of my mouth, but the dark, bitter taste makes up for it.

I lean back into the mattress, exhausted. "I'm sorry, Auggie." My apology is whispered and is as weak as it sounds. I've royally screwed up my reputation and my job with the FBI. Nothing like a botched, off-the-books investigation to do that to a girl.

"For what?"

His response confuses me.

"For all of this."

An audible sigh brings my attention to him. He places his coffee on my meal table and rubs his hands up and down his thighs, head lowered. It's a move I've seen before. He's agitated.

He finally stills, and his eyes seek out mine. "No, Jamie. I'm the one who should be sorry. You're good at what you do, and I know that. Just because I couldn't see what you were seeing ... I shouldn't have belittled it." He runs a hand through his hair. "I should've listened. You're one hell of an analyst, and your intuition is dead-on every time. Every time. So, I don't have any excuse as to why I disregarded it."

I nod. It's good to hear, but he's wrong. I got it wrong this time. So very wrong.

"I'm not sure about that. I didn't get much right while I was here."

His lips purse as he crosses his arms and sits back into the chair. "Yes. Tell me what happened. I only got half of the story from the sheriff. Let's start with last night and how you were found, suffocating with a pillow over your head."

I start from the beginning, explaining how I took my investigation rogue months ago. Taking reports home and working on my research and analysis after hours. How it became like an obsession to me. My decision to visit Dark Hollow Lake under the guise of a vacation, but with the intent to chase down the clues I'd found at the last victim's house—one I had no authorization to be at. Luke. The sheriff. Xander. Jay. Conners. Ratchet's Pass and finally the bonfire.

"Something was slipped into my drink. I worked that out before we left," I say. "But I thought it was Conners. He was acting weird and said some things I took as a threat. He sounded like the killer."

I rub my head and close my eyes, trying to recall all of the facts. "But it was Jay. I didn't put two and two together until I saw the rope in his car. I remember when we got to the cabin, my hands had already been tied. Jay went inside for some reason, and I managed to get my cell phone out of my pocket and tried to call the sheriff. He didn't pick up."

"You know Conners was the one to find you?" Auggie says, watching my reaction.

"No. I don't have any clear memories of anything after …" I gingerly touch the side of my mouth, wondering if the bruising from where Jay hit me was showing. "Conners knew about Dawn. He knew she had been murdered and suspected Jay. I can see that now."

Auggie nods, not at all surprised with my conclusion and confirming my hunch.

"Conners suspected Jay for a while but didn't quite work out the whole picture. He didn't know about the others. He was playing it close to his chest because he realized the town was skewed with its perception toward Jay."

"That makes sense," I say slowly. "And he tried to warn me off Jay, thinking I was here, looking for some sort of fling. Or when my intentions became a bit more obvious, to try to get me to stand down."

"We should be lucky you are an amazingly skilled analyst, as your field skills are severely lacking," Auggie says, deadpan, and I groan, the fear of losing my job again at the fore of my mind.

"Am I going to be fired?" I ask quietly. "I know how much I fucked up."

His nose flutters as he exhales audibly, tapping a finger on his chin. "Since you're the only one who knows how the electronic filing system works and the new analyst is getting on my nerves … I think your job is safe for now—under one condition."

"Which is?"

"You never go off-the-books again."

Looking down at my bruised and battered body, I agree that is a condition I am willing to keep.

TWENTY-EIGHT

The bed in the cell is cold and hard. Mottled stains mar the ceiling, creating unsymmetrical watermarked patterns across the surface. An itch forms on the palm of my hand, and my nails rake furiously across it, trying to find relief. The more I scratch, the more it burns.

Next time, I will burn her.

ABOUT THE AUTHOR

K. Moore is the author of domestic psychological thrillers, including *All for Mother*, *Desert Rose*, and a novella in a shared world anthology, *Killer at Dark Hollow Lake*.

She currently resides along Australia's Sunshine Coast with her husband, two sons, and their Karelian bear dog named Hathor. In her free time, she enjoys gardening, hiking along the beach, and reading—about the only things one can successfully do during a global pandemic. If you manage to locate a decent bottle of gin and a chair at the bar, she might be convinced to regale you with tales of her global travels. Without the gin, you'll have to find the evidence within the pages of her stories and poetry.

Find K. Moore online at:

www.AuthorKMoore.com

www.facebook.com/AuthorKMoore

www.instagram.com/runs2ny/

https://twitter.com/runs2ny

Keep up-to-date and sign up for
K. Moore's newsletter: http://bit.ly/kmoorenews